My Amazing Toddler
Behavioral Series

I Share My Toys.
I Am KIND!

By Suzanne T. Christian

TWORAVENS
B O O K S

Two Little Ravens
CHILDREN'S NON-FICTION BOOKS

Paperback Edition: 9781960320995
Hardcover Edition: 9781964202006
Digital Edition: 9781964202013

Published in the United States by Two Ravens Books LLC,
254 Chapman Rd, Ste 209, Newark DE 19702

'Expand the mind, free the imagination, one title at a time.'
www.tworavensbooks.com

Welcome to
"I Share My Toys. I Am Kind!"

This book is a delightful collection of easy-to-understand affirmations designed specifically for young children. As you explore its pages together, your child will learn the importance of kindness, empathy, and positivity.

Each page features vibrant illustrations and relatable scenarios that foster loving and thoughtful interactions. By making this book a regular part of your reading routine, you can witness a gradual improvement in your toddler's behavior, as repetition is a proven teaching tool.

Prepare for a journey of emotional growth, empathy, and lots of fun with your toddler!

Suzanne T. Christian

Sharing toys makes playtime double the fun!

Listening to my teacher
is the right thing to do.

Sharing books with friends
makes stories come alive!

Sharing my crayons
makes art time fun.

When I want a turn,
I say **"please."**

Gentle hands keep everyone smiling.

Helping my friends
is what I do.
I am kind!

Hugs make
everything better.

Saying **"sorry"** is what I do when I make a mistake.

Helping my sibling makes us a team.

Sharing my yummy snacks
is showing kindness!

Kind words are my superpower.
I am kind!

Saying "hello"
to new friends is exciting!

Playing gently
with pets is kind.

When it's time to

Clean Up, Clean Up,

I do my part!

When others talk,
I listen carefully.

Cheering for friends is the best!

Saying **"good job"** spreads happiness.

I say **"I love you"** to my family.

Nice words make friends happy.
I am **kind!**

Saying **"excuse me"**
helps me pass by nicely.

I share my toys.

I am kind!

The End!

My Amazing Toddler Behavioral Series

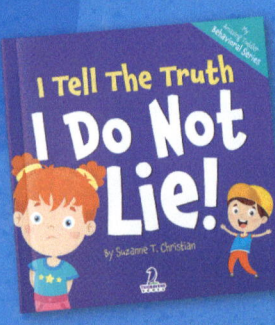

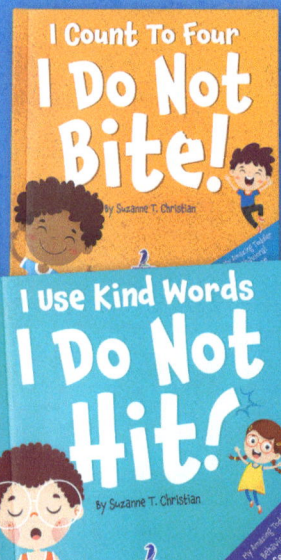

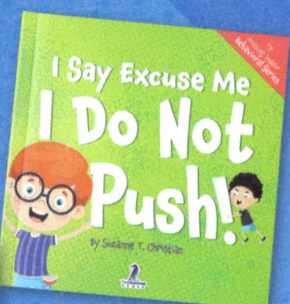

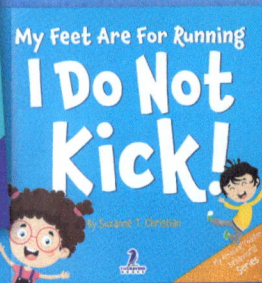

Check Out
Suzanne T. Christian's beloved series
'My Amazing Toddler Behavioral Series'.
Young readers are sure to enjoy!

Two Little Ravens
CHILDREN'S NON-FICTION BOOKS

Dear Amazing Reader,

Thank you for diving into **I Share My Toys. I Am Kind!** with me. If this book touched your heart or made a difference for a young reader, I'd be grateful if you could share your thoughts in a review. Your feedback inspires my future work and helps others discover the magic within these pages.

I'd love to hear from you directly if you have suggestions or ideas for improving the book. Please feel free to reach out to me at **suzanne.christian@tworavensbooks.com.** Your voice counts, and I cherish it deeply.

With heartfelt gratitude,